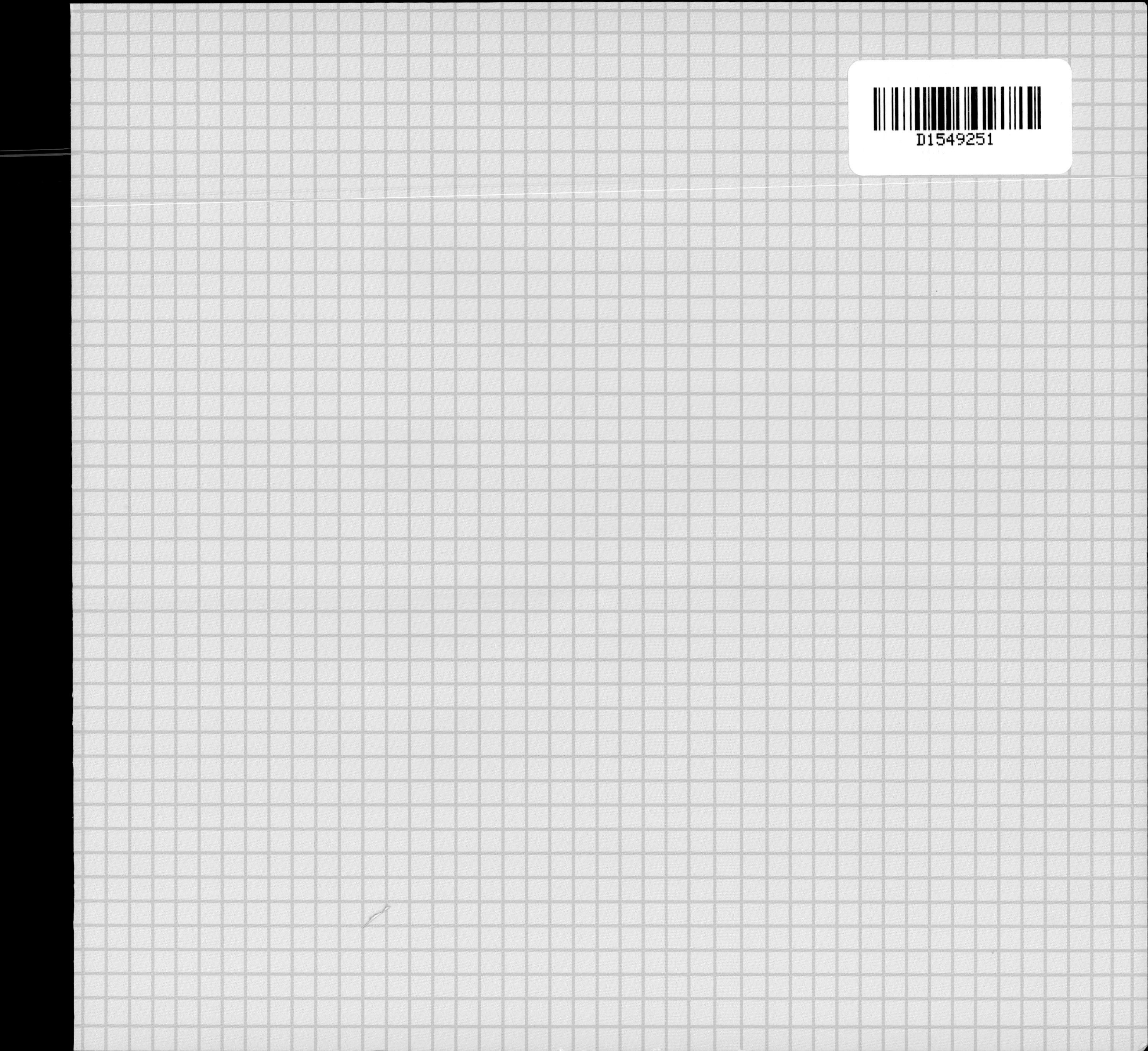

EGMONT
We bring stories to life

First published in Great Britain in 2013
by Egmont UK Limited,
The Yellow Building,
1 Nicholas Road, London W11 4AN

ISBN 978 0 6035 6909 8
56736/1
Printed in Singapore

King of the Mountain

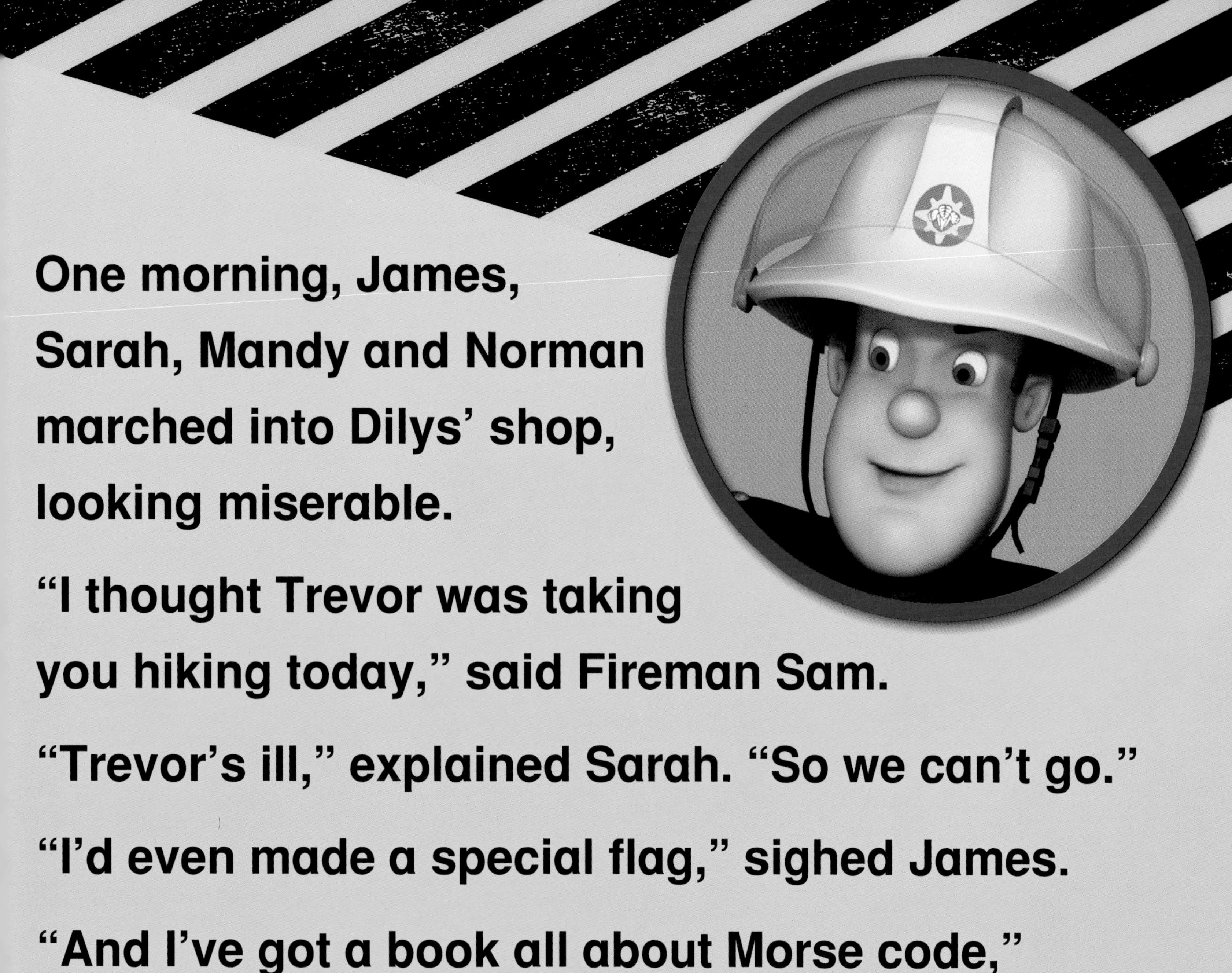

One morning, James, Sarah, Mandy and Norman marched into Dilys' shop, looking miserable.

"I thought Trevor was taking you hiking today," said Fireman Sam.

"Trevor's ill," explained Sarah. "So we can't go."

"I'd even made a special flag," sighed James.

"And I've got a book all about Morse code," said Mandy.

Just then, Moose and Tom walked into the shop. They were getting ready to go on a hike. Tom was boasting about his latest piece of kit – a compass.

"I don't need a compass to find my way around," laughed Moose.

Then Sam had an idea. "You guys could take the kids hiking!"

"Yes, and we could see who knows the most about hiking, eh Moose?" said Tom.

Tom and Moose carried on squabbling as they led the children up into the mountains.

"Maybe this wasn't such a good idea," said Sarah, looking at James.

"Aaaah!" wailed James. "The sun reflecting off your glasses hurts my eyes."

"Sorry," said Sarah, taking her glasses off.

Meanwhile, down at the Fire Station, Elvis was trying out some new tree spurs.

"These will help you climb trees quickly," explained Station Officer Steele. "Perfect for cat rescues."

Elvis hopped up and down in the new boots. He was very pleased with his new kit!

Up in the mountains, things weren't going well. Moose and Tom had got them all lost!

"There's only one thing for it," said Moose. "We'll have to climb a tree to see where we are."

"**Race you**," said Tom. "First to the top is the best mountaineer."

The children watched nervously as Moose and Tom climbed up the tree.

"Get that junk out of my way," grumbled Moose. He was getting caught up in Tom's rope. "Why can't you just use your bare hands?"

Suddenly Moose slipped! The rope tightened around Tom and Moose, tying them to a branch.

The branch creaked and groaned. “This branch is going to break!” said Moose. “Kids, you’d better get help.”

“I can see the Fire Station from here,” cried James.

“We can use my sunglasses to flash a signal,” said Sarah.

“Yes, and we can use Morse code from my book!” added Mandy.

Down at the Fire Station, Elvis and Station Officer Steele saw something flashing in the mountains.

"That's Morse code for SOS," gasped Station Officer Steele. "Someone is in trouble. Sam, you and Penny take Venus. There isn't a moment to lose."

Fireman Sam and Penny arrived at the woods just as the branch was beginning to break.

"We're glad to see you," said Tom, as the branch creaked and groaned.

"**Stand back!**" cried Sam. "I'm going to use the tree spurs."

"But we haven't tested them yet," worried Penny.

"We don't have any choice," said Sam bravely.

Sam put on the tree spurs, and tied a rope to the tree. Then Penny held onto the rope as Sam quickly climbed up the tree.

Sam attached Tom and Moose to the safety line just as the branch gave a final **CRACK** and crashed to the ground!

"Thanks, Sam," gasped Tom.

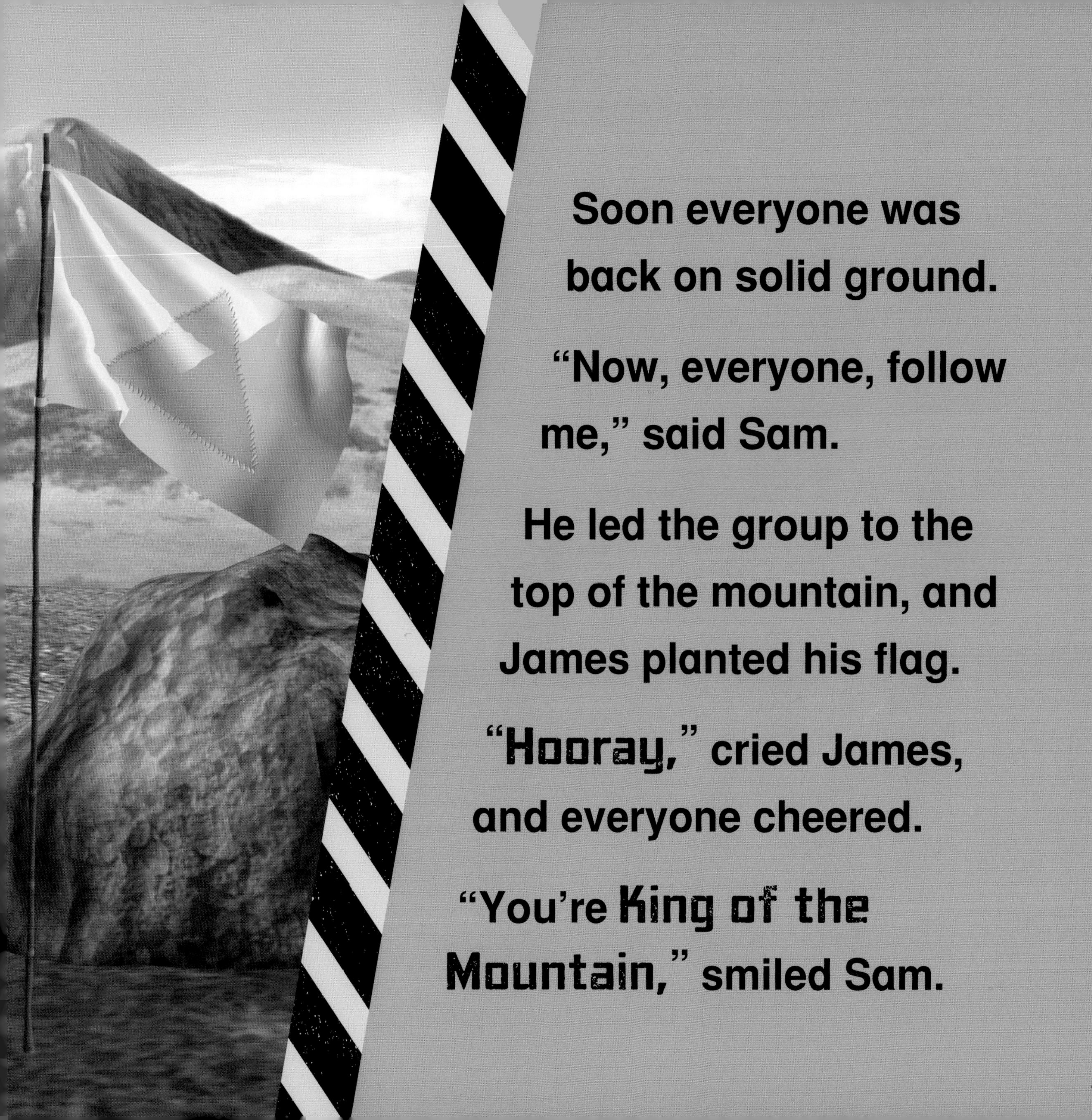

Soon everyone was back on solid ground.

"Now, everyone, follow me," said Sam.

He led the group to the top of the mountain, and James planted his flag.

"Hooray," cried James, and everyone cheered.

"You're King of the Mountain," smiled Sam.

The End